Delbert's
Weekly Workshe
for the
Numeracy Hour

practice, consolidation and evaluation
for homework or classwork

compiled and illustrated
by David Baldwin

Book 2
for Year 4

Contents

Produced
for Badger Publishing
by Nicholas Books

ISBN: 1 85880 676 3
4th impression, 2000

How to Use 'Weekly Worksheets for the Numeracy Hour'

These worksheets are intended to help all teachers in Key Stage 2 to deliver the new requirements of the Numeracy Hour. They follow the key objectives and supplementary guide of the Numeracy programme very closely. They also follow the teaching sequence set out in the Numeracy Hour documentation, so they are in the correct order – for unit 1 use sheet 1, and so on. The level of the work is tied to the National Curriculum Attainment Targets and matched to the KS2 programme of study.

'A homework exercise, or activity at the end of a unit of work, can give you useful information about who has learned what...'

This quote is taken from the recent DFEE publication *The National Numeracy Strategy: Framework for Teaching Mathematics from Reception to Year 6*. These sheets are intended to provide you with such exercises. They are an excellent way of consolidating your teaching. At the end of each unit, give the relevant worksheet to your Year 4 children. You will be giving *them* extra practice in the unit's skills (ideal for homework), and giving *yourself* a means to evaluate how well each child has grasped those skills.

Built-in Evaluation and Reward System

These worksheets have been designed to be flexible, to help you deliver the curriculum as effectively as possible. You may use them as short-term assessments, as class activities to consolidate concepts recently covered, as homework, or a combination of all of these.

As well as providing excellent practical work, they are supported with extra material so you can use them as a formal assessment system. If you intend to use this facility it is vital that you are aware of the *Pupil Evaluation Sheet* copymaster at the back of the book. It provides a monitoring system for an individual's progress through the programme, giving you a place to record a grade to reflect the pupil's performance in each unit. It also sets out page references for further practice on each topic elsewhere in the worksheets. The evaluation process is based on the teaching programme in the Framework, and lists topics within their strands. It does not list every activity, though they are all included in the worksheets themselves. The objectives are being consolidated as your children work through Delbert's maths sheets.

The *Progress Sheet*, at the front of the book, can also be photocopied for you or your children to tick off (or record the date) when the sheets are completed. This, in itself, can be a quick and useful monitoring operation.

Once you have identified the quality of work your pupils are producing, Delbert also gives you the means to reward them for their effort. Four certificate copymasters are included. Choose from: 'Personal Best', 'Supreme Effort', 'Whizz Kid – for high marks' and 'Well Done!'.

A word from the author...

"I have used these types of sheets for some time now, and the cartoon character, Delbert, was born almost 20 years ago. The worksheets are full of fun, yet rigorous in content. They fit well into the informal assessment category recommended in the Framework book from the DFEE. I have used them for end of week class activity and as homework, with equal success. They provide a quick monitoring tool, as you can easily see whether a child has grasped a concept covered in the recent 'unit'.

"I have always had a 'Whizz Kids' section. They are not intended for evaluation purposes, but to challenge the children and make them feel good about themselves - something we should all be promoting.

"Most teachers do not need the Numeracy Programme to show them how to teach maths. I have, though, become increasingly despondent at the lack of relevant materials to teach maths effectively in KS2 and, like many of you, resorted to designing my own classwork/homework sheets. They have served me well, and I hope that they will make meeting the requirements of the Numeracy Programme a little less onerous."

David Baldwin

Head of Duncombe School, Bengeo, Hertfordshire
Previously Maths Co-ordinator at St Anthony's Junior School, Hampstead

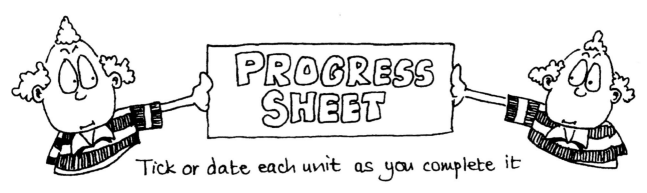

Tick or date each unit as you complete it

Name _____

1 PLACE VALUE

Name _____

No, no Delbert!
Not that kind of
PLAICE!

Each separate number is called a digit. The place where the digit is found tells us what it's worth. This is the PLACE VALUE.

Write down the PLACE VALUE of the underlined digit in each of these:
(The first one is done for you)

1. 3$\underline{4}$7 = $\boxed{40}$

2. 17$\underline{6}$ = ☐

3. $\underline{9}$84 = ☐

4. 18$\underline{7}$5 = ☐

5. 500$\underline{1}$ = ☐

6. $\underline{2}$507 = ☐ ☐

7. 7$\underline{6}$54 = ☐

8. 2$\underline{0}$0 = ☐

9. 9$\underline{7}$1 = ☐

10. $\underline{1}$111 = ☐

11. 561$\underline{2}$3 = ☐

12. 2$\underline{5}$139 = ☐

Put these digits together to make the LARGEST number possible: (The first one is done for you)

13. 3 9 ^{7} = $\boxed{973}$

14. 6 $_2$ ^{8} = ☐

15. 0 $_1$ 6 = ☐

16. 2 ^{4} 6 = ☐

17. 1 ^{05} $_6$ = ☐

18. 8 ^{7} 9 ^{4} = ☐

19. 1 ^{39} $_7$ = ☐

20. ^{7} 6 ^{51} $_9$ = ☐

Brilliant!

WHIZZ KIDS ONLY :

729013 ← re-arrange these digits to make the SMALLEST number ☐

2 PLACE VALUE 2

Name _____

A number is only worth something when we know it's place. The digit 3 may be worth 3, 30, 300 or even 3 000 000! You see?

Now try these:

1. What is the figure 4 worth in the number 6493?

2. What is the figure 7 worth in the number 27052?

3. 6793 = [   ] + 700 + 90 + 3   What number is missing?

4. Write the number that is equivalent to (the same as) in figures: Six thousands, two hundreds and five ones.

5. Write the number that is equivalent to: eight thousands, four tens and one unit.

6. Which is more: 6 hundreds or 61 tens?

7. Which is less: Nine hundreds or eighty-eight tens

8. What needs to be added/subtracted to change 597 to 897?

9. What needs to be added/subtracted to change 9781 to 3781?

I'm glad you're doing these!!!

10. Write these figures in words:
a) 350 = _____
b) 6005 = _____
c) 8400 = _____

11. Write these words in figures:
a) Two thousand, five hundred and twelve
b) Ten thousand, two hundred and three

WHIZZ KIDS ONLY:
Make the smallest number with these digits: 3, 2, 4, 5, 0. Write your answer in words: _____

3 Ordering and Estimating

Name _____

1. On Monday, Delbert walks 5216 metres. On Tuesday, he walks 5616 metres.
   a. On which day did Delbert walk further? ☐

   b. By how much? ☐

2. On Wednesday, Delbert walked a distance greater than (>) 6500 metres, but less than (<) 6700. What distance could it have been? ☐

3. Put these numbers in order, starting with the smallest:
   4621, 6241, 2614, 4162, 2461   ☐, ☐, ☐, ☐, ☐

4. 4520 < ☐ < 4600. What number could ☐ be? ☐

5. A book weighs between 2090 grams and 2110 grams. How heavy could it be? ☐ grams.

6. A painting is valued between £5900 and £6100. What could it be worth? £ ☐

7. Fill in the number indicated here: ☐

   3000 ————————↓———————— 3100

8. Fill in the missing numbers on this number line:
   ☐ 2598 2599 ☐ ☐ ☐

9. ESTIMATE:
   The number shown on this line: ☐
   0 ————↓———— 100

10. ESTIMATE:
    The number shown on this display: ☐

WHIZZ KIDS ONLY:
   Estimate how many words (not numbers) there are on this page. ☐

4 ESTIMATION

Name _____

A. Delbert asks:
Can you round 419 to the nearest 10 ? ☐

B. Now can you round 419 to the nearest 100 ? ☐

I can't believe the size of that THING! It must be roughly 50 metres long, I would guess. Wow!

Sometimes, we need to work with difficult numbers. You will find it easier if the numbers were made simple. Let me give you an example.

$32 \times 19 = \boxed{?} \leftrightarrow 30 \times 20 = \boxed{}$

32 x 19 is roughly the same as 30 x 20

THIS IS TOUGH!

THIS IS EASY!

FIND ESTIMATES (and do the answers) FOR THESE : The first one is done for you.

1. $39 \times 21 = \boxed{40} \times \boxed{20} = \boxed{800}$ 2. $18 \times 19 = \boxed{} \times \boxed{} = \boxed{}$

3. $62 \times 9 = \boxed{} \times \boxed{} = \boxed{}$ 4. $48 \times 12 = \boxed{} \times \boxed{} = \boxed{}$

5. $98 \times 11 = \boxed{} \times \boxed{} = \boxed{}$ 6. $63 \times 29 = \boxed{} \times \boxed{} = \boxed{}$

7. $79 + 39 + 18 = \boxed{} + \boxed{} + \boxed{} = \boxed{}$

8. $299 \div 6.1 = \boxed{} \div \boxed{} = \boxed{}$

9. $495 - 199 = \boxed{} - \boxed{} = \boxed{}$

10. $305 + 194 - 347 = \boxed{} + \boxed{} - \boxed{} = \boxed{}$

WHIZZ KIDS ONLY :

Estimate (a good guess) the answer to : $987 - 594 = \boxed{}$

5 NEGATIVE NUMBERS

Name _____

_____

The measurements on a thermometer show TEMPERATURE. This SCALE is a NUMBER LINE.

When it is very cold, the temperature drops to BELOW ZERO (less than 0)

These numbers are called NEGATIVE NUMBERS.

'O' is FREEZING POINT !

−6 is six degrees below that !

Write the NEGATIVE NUMBERS shown on these thermometers:

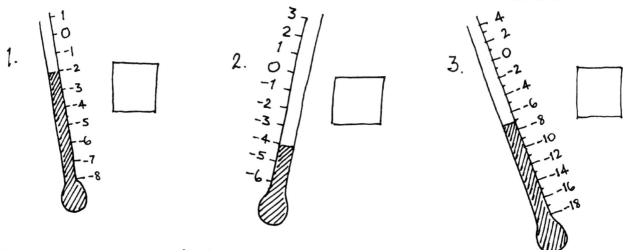

1.   2.   3.

This is another type of thermometer:

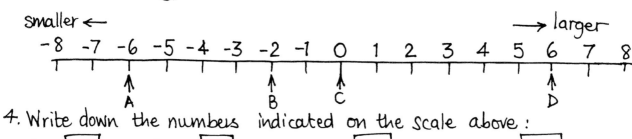

smaller ←   → larger

−8 −7 −6 −5 −4 −3 −2 −1 0 1 2 3 4 5 6 7 8

A   B   C   D

4. Write down the numbers indicated on the scale above:

A = ☐   B = ☐   C = ☐   D = ☐

WHIZZKIDS ONLY : On the thermometer above, show —4 with an arrow.

6 SEQUENCES & MULTIPLES

Name _____

_____

Actually, I love Hopskotch. Do you?

Delbert is playing Hopskotch with a difference. He only plays on the multiples of 2 (even numbers)

1. Can you name them up to 10? ☐ ☐ ☐ ☐ ☐

2. What number is the highest odd one before 10? ☐

3. Which odd number comes just before 100? ☐

4. Which even number comes immediately before 300? ☐

Fill in the missing numbers in the following sequences:

5. ☐ , ☐ , 48 , 52 , ☐ , 60 , 64 , ☐ , ☐

Well done!

6. 29 , ☐ , 43 , ☐ , 57 , 64 , ☐ , ☐

Predict the next three numbers : 7. 117 , 108 , 99 , ☐ , ☐ , ☐

8. Choose two odd numbers : ☐ ☐ Now add them = ☐

Is this answer also odd? Or is it even? ☐ Does it always happen? ☐

9.

3	8	20
28	32	45
48	60	64

Look at the numbers in this box. Now write all the multiples of 4 on the line below.

_____

10. Now list all the multiples of 8 from the same box _____

11. John has a bag full of marbles. (Lucky boy!) He counts them in 4's and has 1 left over. He then counts them again in 5's and has 3 left over. Can you tell how many marbles John has? ☐

12. There is a special number in the box below that is a multiple of 2, 3, 4, 5 and 10. Can you spot it?

8	16	20	25
30	36	40	50
60	100	101	105

Wow! That is TOUGH!

Answer = ☐

WHIZZ KIDS ONLY: Delbert thinks of a number. His number is less than (<) 30. It is a multiple of 2, 3, 4, 6, 8 and 12. Can you name it? ☐

7 FRACTIONS

Name _____

Look at Delbert's flag

Now, answer these questions:

1. The flag is divided into how many squares? ☐

2. What do we call each part? ☐

3. How many 'parts' are shaded on his flag? ☐

4. How would we write this as a <u>fraction</u>? a.☐ Any other way? b.☐

Can you recognise these fractions: (The first one is done for you)

5. 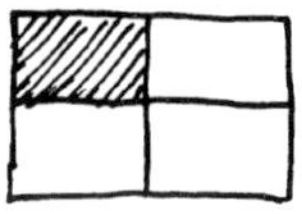 ☐ = $\frac{1}{4}$ 6. 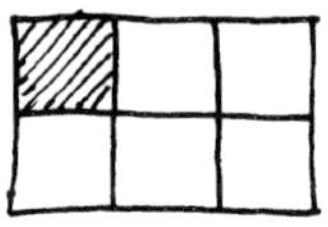 ☐ = ☐   7. 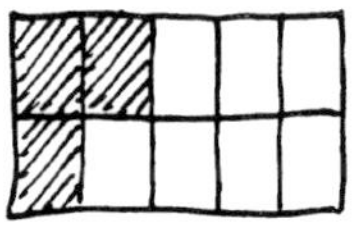 ☐ = ☐

8. 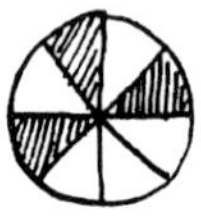 ◯ = ☐   9.  ☐ = ☐   10. 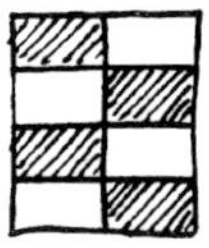 ☐ = ☐   11.  ◯ = ☐

12. On the grid shown on the right, I would like you to shade in $\frac{1}{4}$. Now shade in <u>another</u> $\frac{1}{4}$. Now shade in $\frac{3}{8}$. Now shade in another $\frac{1}{8}$. What have you got?

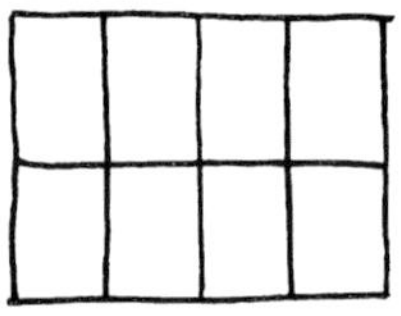

13. 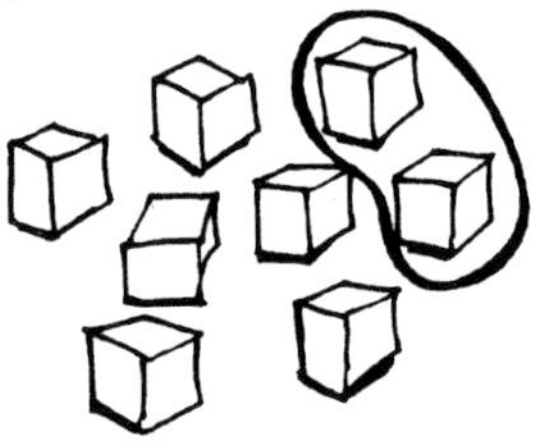 How much (as a fraction) is ringed from the set of cubes? ☐ or ☐   keep going!

14. 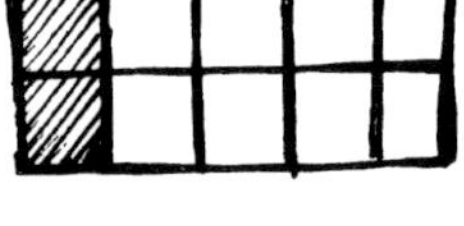 This is $\frac{2}{10}$. Can you write it another way? ☐

15. 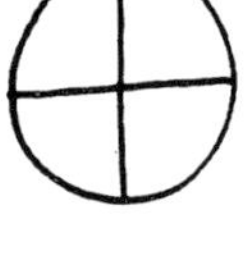 Shade $\frac{3}{8}$ of the circle

16. 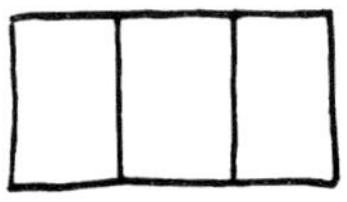 Shade $\frac{5}{6}$ of this rectangle

17.  How much of this circle is shaded? ☐ or ☐

18. Put these fractions in order: (smallest first)
$\frac{1}{2}$, $\frac{1}{4}$, $\frac{3}{4}$, $\frac{1}{8}$, $\frac{7}{8}$

☐ , ☐ , ☐ , ☐ , ☐

WHIZZ KIDS ONLY: Delbert eats $\frac{7}{12}$ of a full packet of crisps. How much is left now? ☐

8 FRACTIONS 2

Name _____

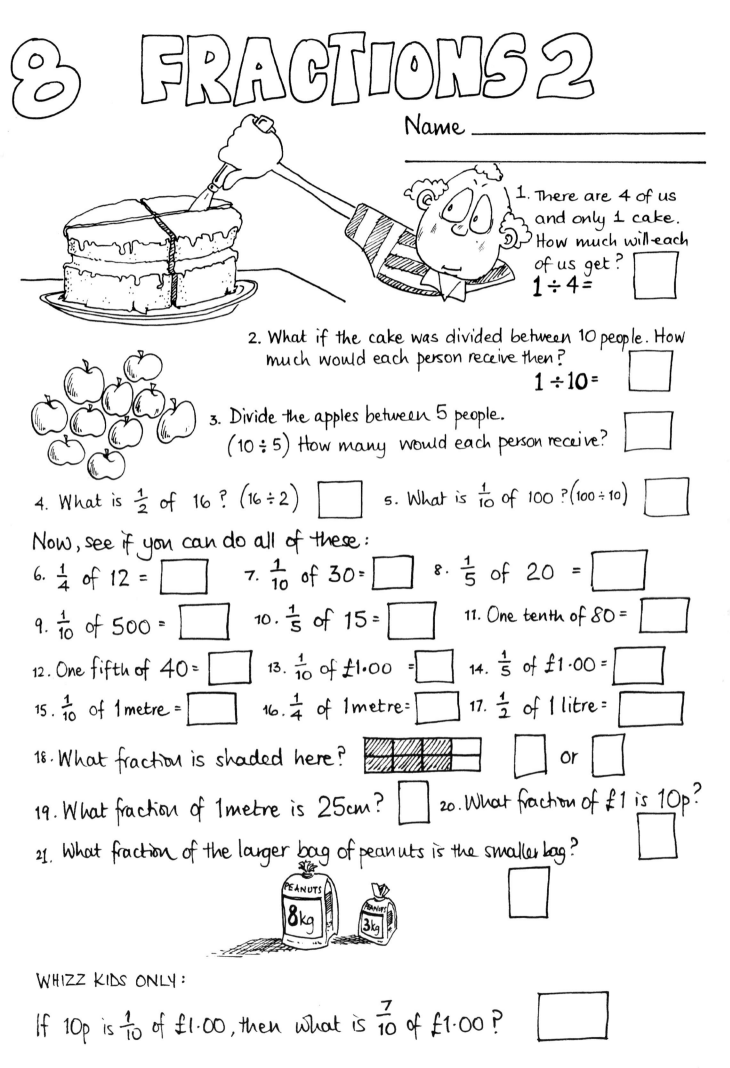

1. There are 4 of us and only 1 cake. How much will each of us get? ☐

   $1 \div 4 =$

2. What if the cake was divided between 10 people. How much would each person receive then? ☐

   $1 \div 10 =$

3. Divide the apples between 5 people. $(10 \div 5)$ How many would each person receive? ☐

4. What is $\frac{1}{2}$ of 16 ? $(16 \div 2)$ ☐

5. What is $\frac{1}{10}$ of 100 ? $(100 \div 10)$ ☐

Now, see if you can do all of these :

6. $\frac{1}{4}$ of 12 = ☐

7. $\frac{1}{10}$ of 30 = ☐

8. $\frac{1}{5}$ of 20 = ☐

9. $\frac{1}{10}$ of 500 = ☐

10. $\frac{1}{5}$ of 15 = ☐

11. One tenth of 80 = ☐

12. One fifth of 40 = ☐

13. $\frac{1}{10}$ of £1·00 = ☐

14. $\frac{1}{5}$ of £1·00 = ☐

15. $\frac{1}{10}$ of 1 metre = ☐

16. $\frac{1}{4}$ of 1 metre = ☐

17. $\frac{1}{2}$ of 1 litre = ☐

18. What fraction is shaded here? ☐ or ☐

19. What fraction of 1 metre is 25cm? ☐

20. What fraction of £1 is 10p? ☐

21. What fraction of the larger bag of peanuts is the smaller bag? ☐

WHIZZ KIDS ONLY :

If 10p is $\frac{1}{10}$ of £1·00, then what is $\frac{7}{10}$ of £1·00 ? ☐

9 DECIMALS

Name _____

_____

What's the point in THAT?

$34 \cdot 7$

Just as we understand that there are whole numbers (Hundreds, Tens and Units) we must understand that there are numbers in-between. These are fractions. (They are numbers worth less than 1 but more than 0.

Decimals (or decimal fractions, as we should say) sort out these numbers into COLUMNS, so it is easy for us to read. Just like H, T, U in whole numbers, we have Tenths ($\frac{1}{10}$'s) and Hundredths ($\frac{1}{100}$'s) in Decimals. Oh, yes; The whole numbers are separated from decimals with a DECIMAL POINT (·) $34 \cdot 7$ means 34 and $\frac{7}{10}$. Got it?

Now try these: (The first one is done for you) 1. $2 \cdot 7 = \boxed{2\frac{7}{10}}$

2. $3 \cdot 9 = \boxed{}$ 3. $4 \cdot 1 = \boxed{}$ 4. $80 \cdot 3 = \boxed{}$

Now try this: 5. Write the decimal fraction for One and four-tenths $\boxed{}$

6. Write $3\frac{7}{10}$ as a decimal fraction: $\boxed{}$

7. Write $57\frac{9}{10}$ as a decimal: $\boxed{}$

Now I see!

Now do these, if you can: (The first one is done)

8. What is the difference between $7 \cdot 3$ and $7 \cdot 5$? $\boxed{0 \cdot 2 \text{ or } \frac{2}{10}}$

9. What is the difference between $1 \cdot 9$ and $1 \cdot 3$? $\boxed{}$

10. What is the difference between $0 \cdot 8$ and $0 \cdot 1$? $\boxed{}$

11. Try to complete this decimal number line:

$\boxed{0}-\boxed{0 \cdot 1}-\boxed{0 \cdot 2}-\boxed{0 \cdot 3}-\boxed{}-\boxed{}-\boxed{0 \cdot 6}-\boxed{}-\boxed{0 \cdot 8}-\boxed{}-\boxed{1}-\boxed{1 \cdot 1}-\boxed{}-\boxed{}$

12. Put these in order of size: (start with the smallest)

$7 \cdot 6$, $3 \cdot 7$, $0 \cdot 5$, $3 \cdot 1$, $1 \cdot 1$ $\boxed{},\boxed{},\boxed{},\boxed{},\boxed{}$

13. Try to fill in all the decimals indicated on the number line below.

WHIZZ KIDS ONLY: How would you write 145p as £'s? $\boxed{}$

10 ADDITION

Name_____

Your sums are wrong! I asked for a TAKE AWAY!

Okay, here we go. Let's see just how well you can do with this sheet.

1. $31 + 18 = \boxed{} + 31$

2. Is $32 + 15 + 47$ the same as $15 + 32 + 47$? $\boxed{}$

3. Is $76 + 98 + 34$ the same as $98 + 34 + 76$? $\boxed{}$ How do you know?

4. $37 + 14 = \boxed{}$

5. $\boxed{} + 48 = 67$

6. Increase 250 by 46 $\boxed{}$

7. Add 34 to 89 $\boxed{}$

8. The opposite (INVERSE) to adding is $\boxed{}$

9. $9 + 3 = \boxed{} - 3$

10. $25 + 17 = \boxed{}$ $42 - 17 = \boxed{}$

11. $100 - 45 = \boxed{}$ $45 + \boxed{} = 100$

12. $\boxed{} + 49 = 71$

13. $48 + \boxed{} + 32 = 110$

14. $900 + 150 = \boxed{}$

15. $58p + 60p + 13p + 3p = \boxed{}$

16. $7 + 6 = 13$. So what is $70 + 60$? $\boxed{}$

17. $8 + 7 = 15$. So what is $80 + 70$? $\boxed{}$

18. What is $800 + 700$? $\boxed{}$

19. $45 + \boxed{} = 100$

20. $450 + \boxed{} = 1000$

21. $35 + 35 = \boxed{}$

22. $29 + 29 = \boxed{}$

23. $250 + 250 = \boxed{}$

24. $480 + 480 = \boxed{}$

25. $1500 + 1500 = \boxed{}$

26. $3600 + 3600 = \boxed{}$

That was tough!

27. $850 + \boxed{} = 1000$

28. $720 + \boxed{} = 1000$

29. $350 + \boxed{} = 1000$

30. $190 + \boxed{} = 1000$

WHIZZ KIDS ONLY :

Whose shopping list totals most?

DELBERT'S LIST
Dozen apples £1·40
Book   £4·90
Scarf   £2·75

TOTAL = _____

EGBERT'S LIST
Picture   £2·99
Hat   £3·00
gloves   £2·50

TOTAL = _____

HERBERT'S LIST
Cup   £1·50
Saucer   £1·20
Plate   £2·95
Spoon   £0·99

Total = _____

Ans = _____

11 ADDING 2

25+63? How do **You** do it?

25+63? In my head? Well, I could do: 20+60 = 80 and 5+3 = 8

80 + 8 = 88

— OR —

25 + 60 = 85 and 3 = 88.

Use both these methods to help you do these :

1. 48 + 33 = ☐   2. 26 + 58 = ☐   3. 146 + 48 = ☐

How do you do 36 + 37? Well I know that 36 + 36 = 72 ...... So, 36+37 must be 1 more than that! 36+37 = 73 See if you can do these in the same way: 4. 42 + 43 = ☐   5. 60 + 61 = ☐

6. 250 + 254 = ☐   7. 75 + 77 = ☐   8. 320 + 328 = ☐

Ask your teacher for other ways to do these:

9. 73 + 59 = ☐   10. 254 + 29 = ☐   11. 71 + 48 = ☐

Now, quickly do these sums: 12. 7 + 8 + 3 = ☐   13. 19+8+4 = ☐

14. 28 + 3 + 12 + 7 = ☐   15. 600 + 500 = ☐   16. ☐ + 30 = 100

17. 80 + ☐ = 200   18. 700 + ☐ = 1300   19. 68 + 31 = ☐

20. 3000 + 1518 = ☐   21. 690 + 20 = ☐

Well done! Keep it up.

22. What must I add to 780 to make 900? ☐

23. What is added to 7300 to make 8001 ? ☐

24. Using the numbers 75, 32, 19 and 41, write as many different addition sums as you can.

25. What is 10 more than: a. 3485 ☐   b. 4599 ☐   c. 6010 ☐

26. What is 1000 more than: a. 2780 ☐   b. 50 ☐   c. 105 ☐

WHIZZ KIDS ONLY :
Find the sum of £2·99, £1·95 and £7·06 ☐

12 ADDING 3

Why can't I just use this?

Name _____

_____

I wonder if you can complete the whole of this sheet without a calculator?

Try these in your head:

1. 3500 + 501 = ▢

2. 459 + 70 = ▢

3. 3576 + 9 = ▢

4. 4728 + ▢ = 4736

5. 7109 + 25 = ▢

Sometimes the sums are just too big to do in your head. Look at how Delbert works this out: 368 + 75

```
  H  T  U
  3  6  8
+    7  5
─────────
     1  3   - He adds 8 and 5
  1  3  0   - He adds 60 and 70
+ 3  0  0   - He adds 300 (and 000)
─────────
  4  4  3   - He totals his answers.
```

You don't need to do it this way.
Use your methods to do these:

6.
```
  784
+  43
```

7.
```
  382
+  85
```

8.
```
  197
+  98
```

Well done!

9.
```
  367
+  86
```

10.
```
  488
+  73
```

11.
```
  149
+  92
```

And the same for these money questions:

12.
```
 £4·65
+£3·26
```

13.
```
 £8·17
+£1·39
```

14. Before you finish, can you do this one? 84 + 262 + 4 + 54 ▢

WHIZZ KIDS ONLY: Work out £3·52 + £2·69 + £0·52 ▢

13 SUBTRACTION

Name_____

_____

Okay. Here we go again. Let's see how you can do with these:

1. Is $42 - 19$ the same as $19 - 42$? ☐

2. $5276 - 0 =$ ☐

3. $13 + 12 = 25$. $25 - \boxed{} = 12$

4. $46 + 44 = 90$. $90 - 46 =$ ☐

No. I said "Minus 2"

5. The opposite (INVERSE) to subtraction is ☐ 6. $9 + 3 = 15 - \boxed{}$

7. What is 100 less than 258? ☐   8. Decrease 72 by 56 ☐

9. $48 - 13 = \boxed{}$ 10. $\boxed{} - 48 = 50$ 11. $200 - \boxed{} = 55$

12. What is the difference between 219 and 156? ☐

13. $15 - 6 = 7$. So what is $150 - 60$? ☐ 14. What is $1500 - 600$? ☐

15. $900 - 150 = \boxed{}$ 16. $3001 - 2995 = \boxed{}$ 17. $2005 - 9 =$ ☐

18. $58 - 19 = 39$. Use this fact to work out $580 - 190$ ☐

19. $5800 - 1900 =$ ☐   20. $58 - 20 + 1 = \boxed{}$ 21. $580 - 200 + 10 =$ ☐

22. Use the numbers 20, 40 and 60 to write down as many different subtraction sums as you can.

23. $76 - \boxed{} = 36$.   24. $\boxed{} - 80 = 32$ 25. $205 - \boxed{} = 155$

WHIZZ KIDS ONLY:
Put the answers to the following questions in order (smallest first)

$24 - 13$ $46 - 24$ $900 - 880$ $1500 - 470$ $495 - 399$

☐ smallest   ☐   ☐   ☐   ☐ largest

Weekly Worksheets for the Numeracy Hour: Year 4 © Badger Publishing Ltd 199

14 SUBTRACTION 2

Name _____

_____

65 – 34 in my head? Okay,
I could do this:
65 – 30 = $\boxed{35}$ – 4 = 31.

There, that wasn't so bad.
Can you do this one: 98 – 45 ?

1.

Now try these: 2. 49 – 36 = ☐   3. 184 – 132 = ☐

Can you do this one in your head? 4. 300 – 150 – 20 – 8 = ☐

5. And this? 7000 – 4000 – 500 – 250 – 10 = ☐

6. ☐ – 50 = 80   7. 79 – ☐ = 61   8. ☐ – 90 = 1203

9. ☐ – 600 = 900   10. 258 – ☐ = 198   11. 5000 – ☐ = 10

12. 700 – 12 = ☐   13. 150 – 25 = ☐   14. 500 – ☐ = 491

15. ☐ – 8 = 692   16. 803 – 4 = ☐   17. 6000 – 150 = ☐

18. 3956 – ☐ = 3936   19. 2512 – ☐ = 2312

20. 7002 – 10 = ☐   21. 5008 – 9 = ☐   22. ☐ – 10 = 910

23. 3500 – ☐ = 500   24. 72 – 29 = ☐

25. What is the difference between 8 and 800? ☐

26. Subtract 40 from 4000 ☐

27. What is taken from 8001 to make 7300? ☐

You're a star! Well done.

WHIZZ KIDS ONLY:

What is the difference between £7.50 and £19.10? ☐

15 SUBTRACTION 3

Name_____

Delbert wonders whether you can finish the questions on this sheet. They are tough! Try these in your head to get you in the mood: 1. 300 - 210 : ☐

2. 700 - 501 = ☐

3. 3000 - 8 = ☐   4. 5026 - 27 = ☐   5. 7200 - 199 = ☐

Sometimes, the numbers are just too big or awkward to do in your head. Look at how Delbert works this out : 7 2 3 - 1 1 8

	H	T	U				H	T	U		
	700	20	3	'Adjust' to :			700	10	13		
−	100	10	8		→	−	100	10	8		
							600	0	5	= 605	

CAN'T DO !!

Of course, you don't have to do it that way, but it does help if you understand how Delbert has done it. Now try these :

6.   7 6
    − 3 4

7.   9 5
    − 7 2

8.   1 3 5
    − 1 2 0

9.   8 1
    − 4 9

10.   3 1 2
    −   7 0

11.   5 6 7
    −   7 3

12.   9 1 3
    −   9 5

And this money one?   13.   £ 7 · 2 5
                            − £ 2 · 1 8

WHIZZ KIDS ONLY :

4550 − 1234 =   ☐

16 SUBTRACTION 4

Name _____

Yippee!!

See if you can get all the way to the end in Delbert's game.

START

1. $25 - 13 =$
2. $\begin{array}{r} 95 \\ -64 \end{array}$
3. $\begin{array}{r} 239 \\ -135 \end{array}$
4. $500 - 350 =$

5. $36 - 15 =$
6. $\begin{array}{r} 1238 \\ -216 \end{array}$
7. $\begin{array}{r} 956 \\ -408 \end{array}$
8. $\begin{array}{r} 20 \\ -11 \end{array}$

9. $90 = 200 - ?$

10. $900 - 450 =$
11. $105 - 75 =$
12. $36 - 28 =$
13. $\begin{array}{r} 147 \\ -125 \end{array}$
14. $127 - 34 =$

15. $60 - 13 =$
16. $\begin{array}{r} 320 \\ -121 \end{array}$
17. $\begin{array}{r} 340 \\ -180 \end{array}$
18. $\begin{array}{r} 700 \\ -60 \end{array}$

19. $500 - 190 =$

20. $350 - 170 =$
21. $\begin{array}{r} 50 \\ -29 \end{array}$
22. $100 - 56 =$
23. $200 - 156 =$
24. $300 - 256 =$

25. $400 - 356 =$
26. $500 - 451 =$
27. $1000 - 1 =$
28. $5000 - 1 =$

YIPPEE!

You made it..

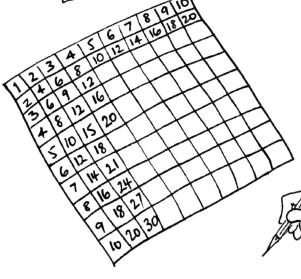

Name _____

HELP!
Please help me
by completing the
Times Table here...
Thanks !!

Now use the table to help

Delbert says that 2 + 2 + 2 + 2 is the same as 2 × 4 !
See if you can work out these multiplication questions :

1. 4 × 2 = ☐

2. 3 × 3 = ☐

3. 4 × 3 = ☐

4. 5 × 3 = ☐

5. 6 × 2 = ☐

6. 3 × 6 = ☐

7. 4 × 4 = ☐

8. 5 × 4 = ☐

9. 7 × 3 = ☐

10. 3 × 8 = ☐

11. 2 × 9 = ☐

12. 3 × 10 = ☐

13. 11 × 4 = ☐

14. 5 × 7 = ☐

15. 6 × 6 = ☐

16. 10 × 10 = ☐

17. 8 × 5 = ☐

18. 7 × 6 = ☐

19. 7 × 7 = ☐

20. 9 × 5 = ☐

That wasn't so bad was it?

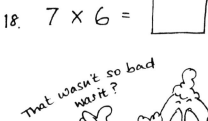

WHIZZ KIDS ONLY :

2 × 2 × 2 × 2 × 2 = ☐

18 MULTIPLICATION 2

Name _____

8x31   31x8

Can you do all of these?

1. 17 × 9 = 9 × ☐   Hee hee!

2. 7 + 7 + 7 + 7 = 7 × ☐

3. The opposite of multiplication is ☐

4. What are six eights? ☐   5. What is double thirteen? ☐

6. Twelve times four = ☐   7. What is the product (×) of 6 and 9? ☐

8. Is 36 a multiple of 9? ☐   9. Multiply 6 by 5 ☐

10. 9 × 4 = ☐   11. 90 × 4 = ☐   12. 4 × ☐ = 48

13. 9 × ☐ = 900   14. 7 × ☐ = 280   15. ☐ × 90 = 720

16. Double all the following: a. 48 → ☐   b. 65 → ☐   c. 350 → ☐

17. 65 × 10 = ☐   18. 65 × 20 = ☐   19. 65 × 40 → ☐

Don't panic!   use this FACT...   to help you to do this.   ....and this!

20. 1 × 15 = ☐ , 2 × 15 = ☐ , 4 × 15 = ☐ , 8 × 15 = ☐

21. Use the facts above (if you can) to do 13 × 15   ☐
                                            ↓
                                        (8 + 4 + 1!)

A CLUE!

22. 32 × 10 = 320. So, what is 32 × 11? ☐

23. 16 × 10 = 160. So, what is 16 × 9? ☐

WHIZZ KIDS ONLY:

Delbert bought 41 pencils at 45p each. How much did he spend altogether? ☐

19 MULTIPLICATION 3

Name_____

Half of 10 is 5, isn't it? Use this fact to work out :

17 x 5 | 17 × <u>10</u> = 170 | = [ ]

Answer at end of sheet.

Now try this: 1. 14 x 5 = [ ]

2. And this: 24 x 5 = [ ]

3. 32 x 10 = [ ]   4. 480 x 10 = [ ]   5. [ ] x 10 = 960

6. 55 x 2 = [ ]   7. [ ] x 2 = 250   8. 18 x [ ] = 36

9. 18 x [ ] = 54   10. 550 = [ ] x 10   11. 29 = 7 x [ ] + 1

12. **35 x 6** can be done like this : (30 x 6) + (5 x 6)
(180) + (30) = 210

Can you do one like this? 32 x 4 = (30 x 4) + (2 x 4)
( ) + ( ) = [ ]

13.   18 x 8 can also be done like this :

×	10	8
8	80	64

= 144   Do this one :

×	20	3
4		

= [ ]

14.   18 x 8 can also be done like this :

```
   18
 x  8
 ----
   64   (8 x 8)
 + 80   (10 x 8)
 ----
  144
```
Ans = | 144 |

Now do this one in the same way:

```
   2 3
 x   6
 ----


 ----

```
Ans = [ ]

WH122 KIDS ONLY :

Can you work out 24 x 7 ?

Ans = [ ]

(Answer 17 x 5 = 85)

20 MULTIPLICATION IV

- Yeehar!

Name_____

_____

Playing with 3 darts, Delbert scores

a. A treble (×3) twenty.........

b. A treble sixteen ....

and c. A double thirteen......

What is his TOTAL SCORE ?

A.

It's mine!

Can you use your skills to try to work all of these out ?

1. What do I get if I multiply 7 with 12 ?

2. Find six times nine

3. What is the product of 8 and 7 ?

4. What are 12 lots of 9 ?

5. Buy 6 tennis balls at 20p each.

DARTS CHAMPION

6. $\begin{array}{r} 65 \\ \times\ 8 \\ \hline \end{array}$

7. $\begin{array}{r} 76 \\ \times\ 3 \\ \hline \end{array}$

8. $\begin{array}{r} 23 \\ \times\ 4 \\ \hline \end{array}$

9. $\begin{array}{r} 64 \\ \times\ 3 \\ \hline \end{array}$

10. $\begin{array}{r} 25 \\ \times\ 3 \\ \hline \end{array}$

11. $\begin{array}{r} 90 \\ \times\ 4 \\ \hline \end{array}$

12. One cup of tea costs 70p at Delbert's Cafe. How much would it cost to buy 8 cups of tea ?

WHIZZ KIDS ONLY:

Try to finish off this strange sequence :

1   2   4   8   16

21 MONEY

Name _____

_____

Delbert has 325 pennies. That's 325p. How can he write this in Pounds and pence?

Well, there are 100p in £1. Delbert has 325p, and that is enough for £3 (300p) with 25p left over. So, Delbert can write 325p like this: £3·25

Try to do these:

1. 215p = ☐

2. 199p = ☐

3. 665p = ☐

4. 401p = ☐

5. 930p = ☐

6. 95p = ☐

The fewest coins needed to make 63p is 4. (50p + 10p + 2p + 1p)

Now try these: (The first one is done for you)

7. List the coins you would need to make 75p. 50p + 20p + 5p

8. List the coins needed for £1·15. ☐ + ☐ + ☐

9. List the coins needed for £3·34. ☐ + ☐ + ☐ + ☐ + ☐ + ☐

10. List the coins needed for £2·79 ☐ + ☐ + ☐ + ☐ + ☐ + ☐

Now try to work these out:

11. Delbert buys a comic for 65p. He pays with a £1 coin. What is his change? ☐

12. Add 15p to these amounts: 12p → ☐   37p → ☐

90p → ☐   £9·09 → ☐

WHIZZ KIDS ONLY: 7 bananas cost £0·84. How much for 2 bananas? ☐

22 MONEY 2

MONEY PROBLEMS OH, NO!

Name _____

Delbert receives 5 bills on Saturday, for £10·50, £20, £55, £3·50 and 99p. How much does this total?

1.

2. He has £100. Is this enough?

3. What's his change? (If any)

4. A whizzo bar costs 29p. How many could I buy with £1? How much change would I receive?

5. Nicola wants to buy a fabulous poster of Delbert. It costs £12. She saves 60p a week. How many weeks must she save?

6. It costs £4·20 for a cinema ticket. How much would 3 tickets cost?

7. Work out the cost of Delbert's shopping ➔

Saturday Shopping

2 dozen eggs (£1·90 per dozen)

3 teddy bears (£5·00 each)

10 Candles (27p each)

TOTAL =

8. Delbert spent one quarter of the money in his piggy bank. What did he spend if the piggy bank had £10?

Oh, no. Not again!

WHIZZ KIDS ONLY:

At Uncle Norman's Toy shop, you receive a £1 voucher for every £20 you spend there. Delbert spent £180 (He has a large family) How much (in vouchers) is he entitled to in return?

23 DIVISION I

DELBERT ÷ 6!

Ever played cards?
Ever been chosen in a team?
If you have, then you already know all about DIVISION. It's all about sharing, grouping.
Have you also noticed that it is similar to FRACTIONS?

Suppose we have 8 apples to share between 2 children. If we divide the 8 apples between 2, we would get 4. So, 8 ÷ 2 = 4!

8 APPLES ÷ BETWEEN 2 PEOPLE = 4 APPLES EACH

Now do these (if you can!):

1. 9 ÷ 3 = ☐   2. 10 ÷ 2 = ☐   3. 12 ÷ 4 = ☐

4. 15 ÷ 5 = ☐   5. 20 ÷ 4 = ☐   6. 24 ÷ 6 = ☐

7. 21 ÷ 3 = ☐   8. 18 ÷ 6 = ☐   9. 28 ÷ 7 = ☐

10. 36 ÷ 4 = ☐   11. 25 ÷ 5 = ☐   12. 36 ÷ 6 = ☐

13. 40 ÷ 10 = ☐   14. 45 ÷ 9 = ☐   15. 32 ÷ 8 = ☐

WHIZZ KIDS ONLY :

A. 84 ÷ 4 = ☐   THAT LOOKS ODD!   B. 72 ÷ 1 = ☐

24 DIVISION 2

Name_____

_____

Divide the Delberts into 4 equal groups, by putting rings around these groups. How many groups are there? **A.** ☐

Are any Delberts LEFT OVER? **B.** ☐ How many? **C.** ☐

Now, let's see if you can do these:

All of these have remainders. The first one is done for you:

1. $17 \div 5 = $ 3 r 2

2. $18 \div 4 = $ ☐

3. $29 \div 3 = $ ☐

4. $32 \div 6 = $ ☐

5. $37 \div 4 = $ ☐

6. $43 \div 7 = $ ☐

7. $701 \div 100 = $ ☐

8. $64 \div 5 = $ ☐

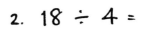

Now try these:

9. Delbert shares 62 cakes equally between 4 people. How many cakes would each person receive? ☐

10. A minibus can take 13 people. How many minibuses are needed to take 56 people to the seaside? ☐

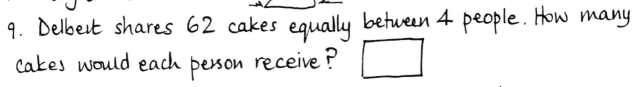

11. Three children shared 96 doughnuts. How many each? ☐

They will be ill!

12. 4 children saved £22. They each saved the same amount. How much did each child save? ☐

WHIZZ KIDS ONLY:
How many lengths of 13cm can be made from 1metre? ☐

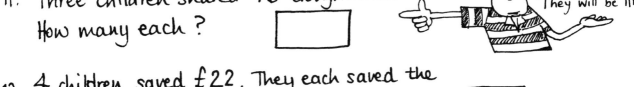

25 DIVISION 3

Name_____

_____

DELBERT

1st TEE

As the teacher says: 'Just concentrate and you'll be fine!'

I wonder if you can complete all of the questions on this worksheet.
Are you ready? Off we go!

1. Share 45 between 6 = ☐

2. Divide 68 by 3 = ☐

3. Give the quotient (÷) of 28 and 4 ☐

4. Give 3 factors of the number 15 ☐ ☐ ☐

5. What is $\frac{1}{4}$ of 12 ? ☐   6. 12 ÷ 4 = ☐   7. How many 3's in 12? ☐

8. Division is the opposite of ☐

9. 1465 ÷ 5 = ☐   10. ☐ ÷ 30 = 8

11. 3 ÷ 4 = ☐   12. 13 ÷ 4 = ☐

13. Half of 8400 = ☐   14. 72 ÷ ☐ = 18

15. How many centimetres in $\frac{1}{4}$ metre ? ☐

16. $\frac{1}{8}$ of 64 (64 ÷ 8) = ☐   17. $\frac{1}{6}$ of 42 = ☐

Anyone spot my ball?

18. 108 x 12 = 1296. So, what is 1296 ÷ 12? ☐

19. Dividing by 10.... a/ 30 ÷ 10 = ☐ b, 700 ÷ 10 = ☐ c/ 7000 ÷ 10 = ☐

20. Dividing by 100.... a/ 300 ÷ 100 = ☐ b, 5000 ÷ 100 = ☐ c/ 10 000 ÷ 100 = ☐

21. Halve these numbers: a/ 76 ☐ b, 900 ☐

WHIZZ KIDS ONLY:

How many times can you buy a first class stamp with £2 ?

☐

26 DIVISION 4

Name _____

When you are going to work out some tough questions, it is ALWAYS a good idea to ESTIMATE first.
Here is an example: $84 \div 5$
Well, $50 \div 5 = 10$. $100 \div 5 = 20$. So, the answer will be somewhere between 10 and 20. Okay?

Now look at this method of division:

$$5\overline{)84}$$
$$-50 \quad \text{because } \textcircled{10} \times 5 = 50$$
$$34$$
$$-30 \quad \text{because } \textcircled{6} \times 5 = 30$$
$$4 \quad \text{So, the answer} = 16 \text{ r } \underline{4}$$

Don't worry if you cannot understand this now.

You will soon

See if you can do all of these examples:

1. $5\overline{)91}$

2. $4\overline{)93}$

3. $6\overline{)97}$

4. $5\overline{)76}$

5. $3\overline{)82}$

6. $7\overline{)99}$

WHIZZ KIDS ONLY: Divide £9.50 between 5 people. How much each? ☐

27 TIME

Name _____

_____

TICK-TOCK

Remember: 60 seconds = 1 minute.
60 minutes = 1 hour.   24 hours = 1 day.
7 days = 1 week.   52 weeks = 1 year.
100 years = 1 century and
1000 years = 1 millennium.

Read this rhyme: '30 days hath September,
April, June and November.
All the rest have 31,
except in February alone.
Which has but 28 days dear
and 29 in each leap year.'

I LOVE LEAP YEARS

Can you write the times shown on the following clocks?

1.

2.

3

4. 23 minutes to 7pm. Write this on a digital clock: [:   ]

5.

WIGAN	10:15	1:30	4:15
BOLTON	10:40	1:55	
MANCHESTER	11:50		5:50
LEEDS		1:05	4:20

Study this timetable. It shows Delbert's magic bus times.

Now try to answer:

A. If you boarded the 1:30 bus from WIGAN, at what time would you arrive in MANCHESTER? [   ]

B. Your bus arrives in LEEDS at 7:05. At what time did this bus stop at BOLTON? [   ]

6. The match started at 7:35pm and lasted 87 minutes. When did it end? [   ]

7. Jane went to bed at 11:40pm on Wednesday, 30th September 1999. She slept for 48 hours and 10 minutes. When (Time, day and date) did she wake up? [   ]

WHIZZ KIDS ONLY:

Gwynneth was born on 27th April 1989. How old is she now? [   ]

28 FUNCTION MACHINES

Name_____

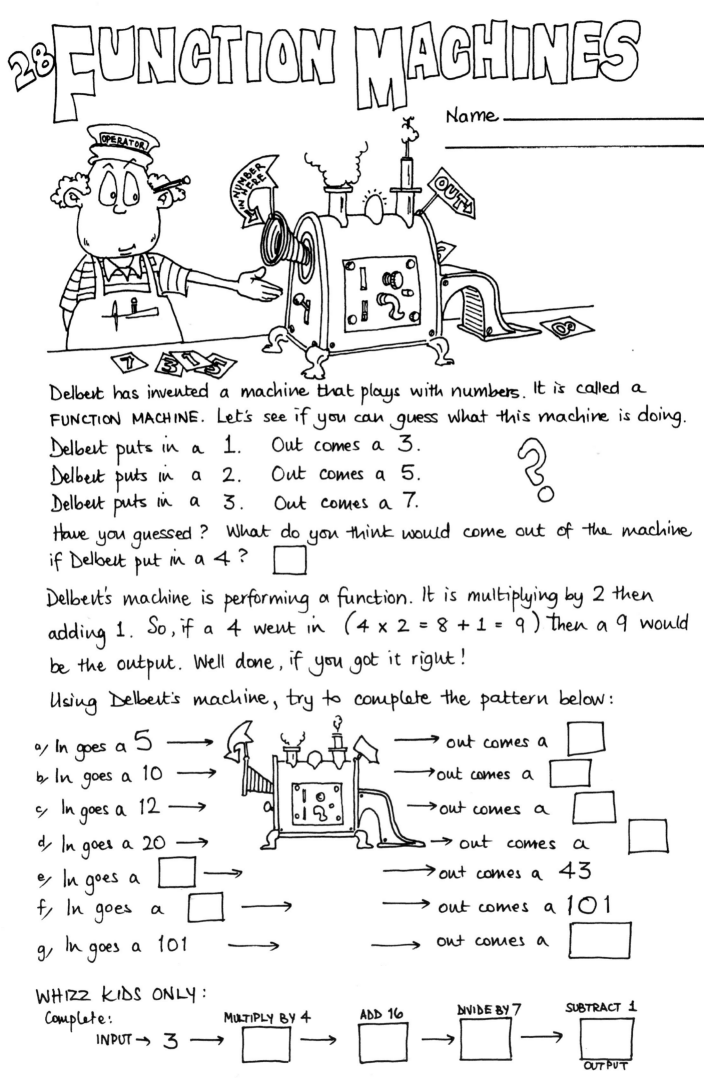

Delbert has invented a machine that plays with numbers. It is called a FUNCTION MACHINE. Let's see if you can guess what this machine is doing.

Delbert puts in a 1. Out comes a 3.
Delbert puts in a 2. Out comes a 5.
Delbert puts in a 3. Out comes a 7.

Have you guessed? What do you think would come out of the machine if Delbert put in a 4? ☐

Delbert's machine is performing a function. It is multiplying by 2 then adding 1. So, if a 4 went in (4 x 2 = 8 + 1 = 9) then a 9 would be the output. Well done, if you got it right!

Using Delbert's machine, try to complete the pattern below:

a/ In goes a 5 ⟶ ⟶ out comes a ☐
b/ In goes a 10 ⟶ ⟶ out comes a ☐
c/ In goes a 12 ⟶ ⟶ out comes a ☐
d/ In goes a 20 ⟶ ⟶ out comes a ☐
e/ In goes a ☐ ⟶ ⟶ out comes a 43
f/ In goes a ☐ ⟶ ⟶ out comes a 101
g/ In goes a 101 ⟶ ⟶ out comes a ☐

WHIZZ KIDS ONLY:
Complete:

INPUT ⟶ 3 ⟶ **MULTIPLY BY 4** ☐ ⟶ **ADD 16** ☐ ⟶ **DIVIDE BY 7** ☐ ⟶ **SUBTRACT 1** ☐
OUTPUT

29 MEASURING

Name_____

_____

*A mile is also used. This is more than 1km, but less than 2km.

Also remember that a pint is roughly the same as half a litre (500ml)

Now try these :

1. 3km = [   ] m

2. ½ km = [   ] m

3. 4·5km = [   ] m

4. 75cm = [   ] m

5. 150cm = [   ] m

6. 3cm = [   ] mm

7. 2500 m = [   ] km

8. 500g = [   ] kg

9. 5000g = [   ] kg

10. 1·6 m = [   ] cm

11. 750mL = [   ] L

12. 1900mL = [   ] L

13. Estimate how heavy your shoe is : [   ]

14. Estimate how tall you are : [   ]

15. Estimate how much water a bucket might hold : [   ]

16. How much water in this measuring cylinder? [   ]

17. Roughly how much is indicated on these scales? [   ]

18. Measure this line.
Write the answer in metres (m) [   ]

WHIZZ KIDS ONLY :

1 mile is roughly 1·6 km. How many metres in 5 miles? [   ]

30 PROBLEMS WITH MEASURES

Name _____

_____

Delbert is proud of his catch. Before he puts it back into the ocean, can you help to measure it?

Estimate its length. (The ruler is marked in centimetres)

1. [ ]

Now try these: 2. Measure these two lines to the nearest mm.

a _____ [ ] mm   b. ⌒⌒ [ ] mm

3. Delbert's fishing rod is in 3 sections, measuring 29cm, 36cm and 45cm. What is the total length of his fishing rod? (in metres) [ ]

4. Delbert's family have already travelled 247 miles of a 516 mile journey. How much further do they still need to travel? [ ] miles.

5. Delbert's brain weighs 250g. How much would 10 brains weigh? [ ]

6. Delbert's overall weight is 50kg. How many times heavier than his brain is that? [ ]

7. A large bottle of shark repellent holds 300 millilitres. How many small (60ml) bottles can be filled from this large bottle? [ ]

8. A bucket holds 3 litres of water. How many 500 millilitre ladles (large spoons) can be filled from this bucket? [ ]

9. What is the PERIMETER (all the way around) of a regular pentagon if one of its sides measures 32cm? [ ]

10. Write 2750 metres as Kilometres [ ]

Well done!

WHIZZ KIDS ONLY:

Delbert walks to John's house (450 metres), to Fred's house (618m), to Jane's (897m) and finally back home (657m). How far did he walk? [ ]

31 PROBLEM SOLVING 1

Name _____

_____

7, 8 and 9 are CONSECUTIVE numbers.
(They follow on in a number line)
They add up to 24. Can you think
of 3 other consecutive numbers

1. that add up to 48? ☐ ☐ ☐

2. Find two numbers that have a sum of 10 and a product of 16.   ☐ ☐

3. ▢ 12 of these cubes could be put together to make
this cuboid : How many cubes for this cuboid?

☐ cubes.

4.
8	3	4
1	5	9
6	7	2

Look carefully at this 'magic' square. What is special about it?

5. Each ◇ represents a missing digit taken from this list: 4, 3, 1, 8

Fill them in: ◇◇ − ◇ + ◇ = 17.   THAT IS TOUGH!

6. Delbert thinks of a 2 digit number. He multiplies
it by 8, and the result is 192. What was his number?   ☐

7. How many triangles can you see
in this shape?

BE CAREFUL!

(There are more than you think!)

☐ triangles

8. Use these numbers (only once) 1, 2, 3, 4, 5, 6, 7, 8, 9 and place them
in these three boxes so that each box has a total of 15.

☐ = 15   ☐ = 15   ☐

WHIZZ KIDS ONLY: I think of a number and then divide it by 15.
My answer is then 10. What was my number?   ☐

Weekly Worksheets for the Numeracy Hour: Year 4   © Badger Publishing Ltd 199

32 PROBLEM SOLVING 2

PRICE LIST:
COD £2.90
CHIPS 80p and £1.20
PIES £1.35
SAUSAGES 70p
PEAS 55p

Name _____

Use all of your brain-power to do this work sheet. Look at the PRICE LIST (Left) Delbert buys: 2 cod, 2 large chips, 1 pie and 2 sausages. What does his bill come to?

1.

Now do these:

1. From a class of 32 children, $\frac{1}{4}$ were absent (school allergy). How many were present?

3. In a games lesson, Mr. Crotchley split the group of 63 up into 3 equal teams. How many in each team?

4. There are 720 people living in Delbertsville. Half of them watch "Southenders" and a third of them watch "Corporation Street". How many of them do <u>not</u> watch either programme?

5. David has 248 worms. Eve has half as many. How many worms do they have altogether?

6. A book shelf has 3 shelves. There are 96 books on the top shelf and 73 books on the bottom shelf. There are 231 books altogether on the bookshelf. How many books on the middle shelf?

7. Delbert thinks of a number, adds 6 and then multiplies it by 3. The answer is 27. What was Delbert's number?

8. Look at this sequence: 2, 7, 12, 17, 22, ... Explain what is happening.

WHIZZ KIDS ONLY: I will be so impressed if you can finish this sequence off:

| J | F | M | A | M | J | J | A | S | | | |

33 MORE PROBLEMS

Name _____

_____

NO PROBLEM!

Now, Let's see if you can really use all of that brain power to answer all of the questions on this sheet.

1. Complete this sequence: 2 , 20 , 200 , ☐ , ☐ , ☐

2. Complete this one (÷ 10) 50 000 , 5000 , ☐ , ☐ , ☐

3. How many times larger is 3600 than 36? ☐

4. How many 10p pieces are there in £10? ☐

5. A can of beans costs 39p. How much for 100 tins? ☐

6. 59 000 ÷ ☐ = 590

7. How many 10's do I need to add on to 263 to get more than 500? ☐

I told you that it wasn't a problem!

8. What is 50g more than 960g? ☐

9. Starting with 3550, how many 100's do I need to add on to get more than 5000? ☐

10. Graveley ⌐→120km—⌐L→ Panktown 260km—⌐L→ Warmly 590km—⌐L→ Blurt 162km—↗ Shtop

How far is it from Graveley to Shtop? ☐

11. Complete this sequence:

| 27 | 23 | 19 | 15 | 11 | 7 | ☐ | ☐ | ☐ | ☐ |

12. Put in order : (smallest first) 7·2 , 2·7 , 2·2 , 7·7 , 0·2

☐ ☐ ☐ ☐ ☐

WHIZZ KIDS ONLY: $0.5 = \frac{1}{2}$, $0.25 = \frac{1}{4}$, 0.75 = ☐

1·75 = ☐

34 MORE PROBLEMS 2

– NO PROBLEM!

Name _____

_____

It looks like Delbert is in trouble again. He will be alright as long as he uses his head.
Now, can you do the same?
Good luck.

1. Odd number + odd number = odd or even? ☐

2. Odd number + even number = odd or even? ☐

3. Large even number − small even number = odd or even? ☐

4. Even number + even number = odd or even? ☐

5. Odd number + odd number + odd number = odd or even? ☐

6. 2 even numbers + odd number = odd or even? ☐

7. Without calculating, can you tell me whether the answer to
   25 + 39 is going to be odd or even? ☐

8. Without calculating, can you tell me whether 28 + 46 + 38 = odd or even? ☐

9. * represents a missing sign (+,−,×,÷,=)
   Can you discover what it is?   90 * 6 = 15   * = ☐

10. * is a missing sign in this one...   85 * 56 = 29   * = ☐

11. One of these numbers: 155·5 , 236·8, 170·4, 160·5, 200 , 130
    goes into the empty box
    in this sum: 140 < ☐ < 160
    Please put it in!

12. How many hours in 1½ days? ☐

EASY!

WHIZZ KIDS ONLY:
180 sausages cost £45·00. How much would 90 sausages cost? ☐

35 AREA and PERIMETER

Name _____

_____

These two shapes are the same : SQUARES.

Yet, they're different sizes aren't they? How do we <u>measure</u> the size of shapes? We do it by looking at the <u>AREA</u> and finding out the space which the shape occupies. Look at this shape:

We <u>can</u> measure its area if we place it on cm squared paper.

Like this

Now all you have to do is <u>count</u> how many centimetre squares there are for the shape. 1. There are [ ] square centimetres.

That's it. That's <u>area</u>!

Now look at this rectangle:

5cm

2 cm   2cm

5 cm

What is its PERIMETER? (That means the distance all the way round the shape)

2. So, how far is it? [ ] cm.

Now try these :   3.   3cm

1cm   1cm   PERIMETER = [ ]

3 cm

4.   3cm   4cm

5cm

The PERIMETER IS [ ]

WHIZZ KIDS ONLY: 2cm

2cm   Draw a rectangle with the same PERIMETER as this square.

36 2-D and 3D

Name _____

Where has my POLLY GONE?

Polygons have 3 or more sides, all straight. A regular polygon has equal length sides and equal size angles.

A rectangle is a regular polygon

This pentagon is not.

Name these polygons: (The first one is done)

1. Pentagon
2.
3.
4.
5.

Now name these: 6.   7.

8. What shape is the face of a 50p piece?

9. Name this solid shape (Polyhedron):

10. Name these polyhedrons:
a.   b.   c.   d.

11. How many cubes would I need to construct this:

12. This is a NET of which polyhedron?

WHIZZ KIDS ONLY:
My solid shape has 5 faces, 6 vertices and 9 edges. Two faces are equilateral triangles.

THIS IS DESCRIBING A _____ ?

37 SYMMETRY

What a beautiful picture!

Name _____

Please sketch the reflection of this shape. The dotted line is the line of symmetry (or mirror line)

1.

2. I have already sketched one line of symmetry onto the square (left) can you sketch the rest?

3. How many lines of symmetry does this semi-circle have? ☐

4. How many lines of symmetry do all the following shapes possess?

a. ☐   b. ☐   c. ☐   d. ☐   e. ☐   f. ☐

g. ☐   h. ☐   i. ☐   j. ☐

WHIZZ KIDS ONLY: ☐ △ ⌓
_ _ _ _ _ _ _ _ _ _ _ _

Draw (sketch) the reflection of the three shapes. The dotted line is the line of symmetry.

38 POSITION and DIRECTION

Name _____

_____

Do you know all your compass points?
Well, here they are:

NORTH

NW   NE

WEST   EAST

SW   SE

SOUTH

TRY TO REMEMBER!

Look carefully at this grid. Now look at the point marked **X**. It has a co-ordinate (plot, position) which is (1,3)

Now look at the point marked **O**. Write the co-ordinate for that point.

1. [ ]

WRITE THE CO-ORDINATES FOR THE POINTS

2 A

3. B

4. C

Put point D on co-ordinate (3,3) and join up dots A→B→C→D→A and colour/shade in the shape.

5. Start at (0,0) and travel NE. List all the co-ordinates you travel through.

[ ]

WHIZZ KIDS ONLY: — BOAT

Which direction must the boat go to reach PORT?

PORT

[ ]

39 ANGLES and ROTATION

Name_____

_____

I'm all in a spin. I don't know which way to go!

360° QUARTER TURN 45° 90° A FULL TURN

A FULL TURN = 360°
HALF A TURN = 180°
QUARTER OF A TURN = ☐°
This angle is called a RIGHT ANGLE.
Half of a right angle = ☐°

Now answer these questions:

1. How many right angles must you do to do a full (360°) turn? ☐

2. Estimate the angles shown:

   a. ☐°   b. ☐°

3. Face WEST. Turn clockwise 180°. In which direction are you facing now? ☐

4. The minute hand is pointing at 1. How many degrees must it turn to point to:

   a/ 2 ☐°   b/ 3 ☐°   c/ 5 ☐°

5. Put these angles in order of size:
   (start with the SMALLEST) 360°, 45°, 30°, 180°, 60° ☐°,☐°,☐°,☐°,☐°

6. Place these angles in order of size (Number smallest 1 and the largest 4)

   120°   90°   ☐   ☐

7. Draw an angle that you estimate roughly as 100°

WHIZZ KIDS ONLY: You face NE. Turn clockwise through 135°. In which direction do you now face? ☐

40 HANDLING DATA

Name _____

_____

Well, you did say that I could handle it!

FAVOURITE SCHOOL DAY

No. of pupils — Days of week (M T W Th F)

Look at the graph here →
Now answer the following questions:

1. 22 people voted Wednesday. Draw in the bar for that day.
2. Which was the least favourite day?
3. Which was the favourite day?
4. How many pupils took part in this graph/survey?

Now look at this **VENN DIAGRAM**:

Rupinder, Sally | Tom, Meggie | Clive, Sandy, Alan

Children in the TENNIS TEAM

Children in the GOLF TEAM

Try to answer these questions.

5. Name the children in the TENNIS TEAM

_____

6. Name the children who are in the TENNIS **AND** GOLF TEAMS:

_____

7. LOOK AT THIS CARROLL DIAGRAM.

	ODD	NOT ODD (EVEN)
Multiples of 3	3 9	6 12
Not multiples of 3	1 5 7	2 4 8 10

This diagram records how some of the whole numbers BELOW 16 were sorted.

Now please add the numbers 11, 13, 14, 15 and 16.

Good luck!

WHIZZ KIDS ONLY: INVENT your own Venn or Carroll diagram. Use the back of this work sheet if you like!

PUPIL EVALUATION SHEET   YEAR 4

Name _____

NUMBERS AND THE NUMBER SYSTEM

: WORKSHEET PAGE NUMBER :

☐ Place value, ordering and rounding   1 2 3 4 33

☐ Negative numbers   5

☐ Properties of numbers and sequencing   6

☐ Fractions   7 8

☐ Decimals   9

CALCULATIONS

☐ Understanding addition and subtraction   10 11 13 14 16

☐ Rapid recall of + and −   10 11 13 14 16

☐ Formal procedures (+ and −)   12 15 16

☐ Understanding multiplication and division   17 18 19 23 24 25

☐ Rapid recall of × and ÷   17 18 20 24 25

☐ Formal procedures (× and ÷)   19 20 25 26

SOLVING PROBLEMS

☐ Making decisions and choices of operation   28 29 31 32 33

☐ Reasoning about numbers and shapes   28 29 31 32 33

☐ 'Real life' problems   21 22 27 30 31 33 34

HANDLING DATA

☐ Organising and interpreting data   40

MEASURES, SHAPES AND SPACE

☐ Measuring (length, mass, capacity, area, perimeter)   27 29 30 35

☐ Shape and space   31 36 39

☐ Symmetry and angles.   37 39

☐ Coordinates   38

Suggested grading: A = Concepts fully understood.
B = Almost there – more practice needed.
C = Not yet understood concepts.

The boxed numbers (eg: 9)
contain highly relevant
materials for assessment.

DELBERT'S

WHIZZ KID AWARD

PRESENTED TO: _____

FOR INCREDIBLY HIGH MARKS IN MATHS!

Signed

DELBERT'S SPECIAL AWARD
TO SAY:

WELL DONE!

Presented to: _____

FOR PROGRESS IN MATHS

Signed

Weekly Worksheets for the Numeracy Hour: Year 4 © Badger Publishing Ltd 1999

DELBERT'S SPECIAL AWARD FOR

SUPREME EFFORT

PRESENTED TO _____

FOR THEIR INDUSTRY IN MATHS

Signed

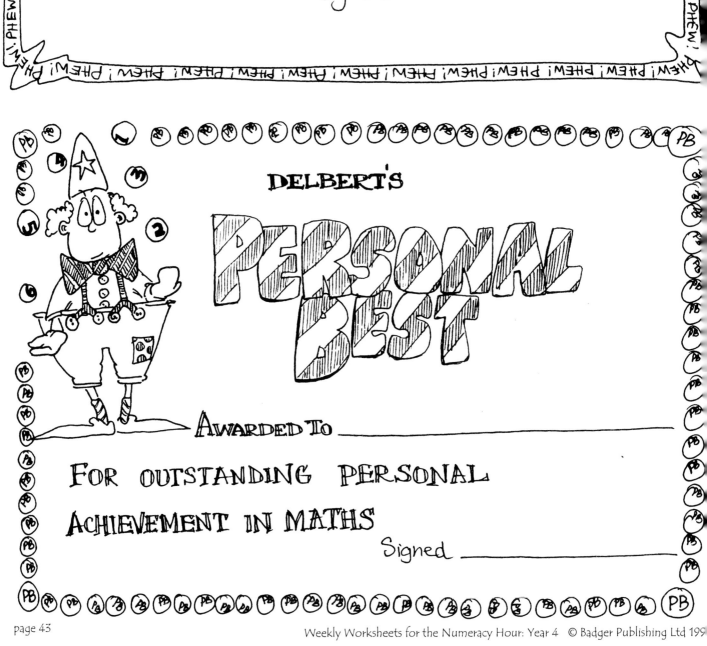

DELBERT'S

PERSONAL BEST

AWARDED TO _____

FOR OUTSTANDING PERSONAL

ACHIEVEMENT IN MATHS

Signed _____

ANSWERS

Sheet

1. 1. – 2. 6 3. 900 4. 70 5. 1 6. 2000 7. 600 8. 0 9. 70 10. 1000 11. 100 12. 5000 13. – 14. 862 15. 610 16. 642
   17. 6510 18. 9874 19. 9731 20. 97651 WK. 012379

2. 1. 400 2. 7000 3. 6000 4. 6205 5. 8041 6. 61 tens 7. 88 tens 8. + 300 9. – 6000 10. a. Three hundred and fifty
   b. Six thousand and five c. Eight thousand, four hundred 11 a. 2512 b. 10 203
   WK. Two thousand, three hundred and forty-five.

3. 1. a. Tuesday b. 400 m 2. Range 6501 - 6699 3. 2461, 2614, 4162, 4621, 6241 4. Range 4521 - 4599
   5. Range 2091 - 2109 g 6. Range £5901 - £6099 7. 3050 8. 2597, 2600, 2601, 2602 9 approx 40 10. approx 440 - 460
   WK. There are 125

4. A. 420 B. 400 1. – 2. 20x20=400 3. 60x10=600 4. 50x10=500 5. 100x10=1000 6. 60x30=1800 7.
   80+40+20=140 8. 300 $\div$ 6=50 9. 500-200=300 10. 300+200-350=150 WK. 400

5. 1. -2 2. -4 3. -7 4a. -6 b. -2 c. 0 d. 6 WK. -4 is indicated

6. 1. 2,4,6,8,10 2. 9 3. 99 4. 298 5. 40,44,56,68,72 6. 36,50,71,78 7. 90,81,72 8. Even,yes 9. 8,20,28,32,48,60,64
   10. 8,32,48,64 11. 13 (or 31,51 etc) 12. 60 WK. 24

7. 1. 10 2. $^1/_{10}$ 3. 5 4a. $^5/_{10}$ b. $^1/_2$ 5. – 6. $^1/_6$ 7. $^3/_{10}$ 8. $^3/_8$ 9. $^4/_8$ or $^1/_2$ 10. $^4/_8$ or $^1/_2$ 11. $^1/_{10}$
   12. 1 (All squares shaded) 13. $^1/_4$ or $^2/_8$ 14. $^1/_5$ 15. 16. 17. $^6/_8$ or $^3/_4$ 18. $^1/_8$, $^1/_4$, $^1/_2$, $^3/_4$, $^7/_8$
   WK. $^5/_{12}$

8. 1. $^1/_4$ 2. $^1/_{10}$ 3. 2 4. 8 5. 10 6. 3 7. 3 8. 4 9. 50 10. 3 11. 8 12. 8 13. 10p 14. 20p 15. 10cm 16. 25cm 17. 500ml
   18. $^6/_8$ or $^3/_4$ 19. $^{25}/_{100}$ or $^1/_4$ 20. $^1/_{10}$ 21. $^3/_8$ WK. 70p

9. 1. – 2. 3$^9/_{10}$ 3. 4$^1/_{10}$ 4. 80$^5/_{10}$ 5. 1.4 6. 3.7 7. 57.9 8. – 9. 0.6 or $^6/_{10}$ 10. 0.7 or $^7/_{10}$ 11. 0.4, 0.5, 0.7, 0.9, 1.2, 1.3
   12. 0.5, 1.1, 3.1, 3.7, 7.6 13. 0.2, 0.4, 0.7, 1.1, 1.7 WK. £1.45

10. 1. 18 2. Yes 3. Yes. Same numbers 4. 51 5. 19 6. 296 7. 123 8. Subtracting (–) 9. 15 10. 42,25 11. 55,55 12. 22
    13. 30 14. 1050 15. £1.34 or 134p 16. 130 17. 150 18. 1500 19. 55 20. 550 21. 70 22. 58 23. 500 24. 960
    25. 3000 26. 7200 27. 150 28. 280 29. 650 30. 810 WK. Delbert's

11. 1. 81 2. 84 3. 194 4. 85 5. 121 6. 504 7. 152 8. 648 9. 132 10. 283 11. 119 12. 18 13. 31 14. 50 15. 1100 16. 70
    17. 120 18. 600 19. 99 20. 4518 21. 710 22. 120 23. 701 24. 75+32=107, 75+19=94, 75+41=116, 32+19=51, 32+41=73,
    19+41=60, 75+32+19=126, 75+19+41=135, 32+19+41=92, 75+32+19+41=167 25a. 3495 b. 4609 c. 6020 26a. 3780 b. 1050
    c. 1105 WK. £12

12. 1. 4001 2. 529 3. 3585 4. 8 5. 7134 6. 827 7. 467 8. 295 9. 453 10. 561 11. 241 12. £7.91 13. £9.56 14. 404
    WK.£6.73

13. 1. No 2. 5276 3. 13 4. 44 5. Addition 6. 3 7. 158 8. 16 9. 35 10. 98 11. 145 12. 63 13. 90 14. 900 15. 750 16. 6
    17. 1996 18. 390 19. 3900 20. 39 21. 390 22. 60-40=20, 60-20=40, 40-20=20, 60-40-20=0 23. 40 24. 112
    25. 50 WK. 11, 20, 22, 96, 1030

14. 1. 53 2. 13 3. 52 4. 122 5. 2240 6. 130 7. 18 8. 1293 9. 1500 10. 60 11. 4990 12. 688 13. 125 14. 9 15. 700
    16. 799 17. 5850 18. 20 19. 200 20. 6992 21. 4999 22. 920 23. 3000 24. 43 25. 792 26. 3960 27. 701 WK.
    £11.60

15. 1. 90 2. 199 3. 2992 4. 4999 5. 7001 6. 42 7. 23 8. 15 9. 32 10. 242 11. 494 12. 818 13. £5.07 WK. 3316

16. 1. 12 2. 31 3. 104 4. 150 5. 21 6. 1022 7. 548 8. 9 9. 110 10. 450 11. 30 12. 8 13. 22 14. 93 15. 47 16. 199
    17. 160 18. 640 19. 310 20. 180 21. 21 22. 44 23. 44 24. 44 25. 44 26. 49 27. 999 28. 4999

17. Tables grid. 1. 8 2. 9 3. 12 4. 15 5. 12 6. 18 7. 16 8. 20 9. 21 10. 24 11. 18 12. 30 13. 44 14. 35 15. 36 16. 100
    17. 40 18. 42 19. 49 20. 45 WK. 32

18. 1. 17 2. 4 3. Division($\div$) 4. 48 5. 26 6. 48 7. 54 8. Yes (4x) 9. 30 10. 36 11. 360 12. 12 13. 100 14. 40 15. 8
    16.a. 96 b. 130 c. 700 17. 650 18. 1300 19. 2600 20. 15,30,60,120 21. 195 (12+60+15) 22. 352 23. 144
    WK. £18.45

19. 1. 70 2. 120 3. 320 4. 4800 5. 96 6. 110 7. 125 8. 2 9. 3 10. 55 11. 4 12. 120+8=128 13. 80+12=92
    14. (Working out) ANS=138 WK. 168

 Weekly Worksheets for the Numeracy Hour: Year 4 © Badger Publishing Ltd 1999

ANSWERS... continued

20. A. 60+48+26=134 1. 84 2. 54 3. 56 4. 108 5. £1.20(120p) 6. 520 7. 228 8. 92 9. 192 10. 75 11. 360 12. £5.60
WK. 32,64,128

21. 1. £2.15 2. £1.99 3. £6.65 4. £4.01 5. £9.30 6. £0.95 7. - 8. £1+10p+5p 9. £2+£1+20p+10p+2p+2p
10. £2+50p+20p+5p+2p+2p 11. 35p 12. 27p,52p,£1.05, £9.24 WK. 24p

22. 1. £89.99 2. Yes 3. £10.01 4. 3 with 13p change 5. 20 6. £12.60 7. £3.80+£15+£2.70=£21.50 8. £2.50 WK. £9

23. 1. 3 2. 5 3. 3 4. 3 5. 5 6. 4 7. 7 8. 3 9. 4 10. 9 11. 5 12. 6 13. 4 14. 5 15. 4 WK. A. 21 B. 72

24. A. 4 B. Yes C. 1 1. - 2. 4 r2 3. 9 r2 4. 5 r2 5. 9 r1 6. 6 r1 7. 7 r1 8. 12 r4 9. 15 (r2) 10. 5 11. 32 12. £5.50 WK. 7

25. 1. 7 r3 (7.5) 2. 22 r2 3. 7 4. From:1,3,5,15 5. 3 6. 3 7. 4 8. Multiplication 9. 293 10. 240 11. Or 3 (³/₄) 12. 3 r1
13. 4200 14. 4 15. 25 16. 8 17. 7 18. 108 19. A.3 B.70 C.700 20. A.3 B.50 C.100 21. A.38 B. 450
WK. (currently, at 26p) 7

26. 1. 18 r1 2. 23 r1 3. 16 r1 4. 15 r1 5. 27 r1 6. 14 r1 WK. £1.90

27. 1. 5:35 (or 25 to 6) 2. 10:55 (or 5 to 11) 3. 2:45 (or Quarter to 3, 15 mins to 3) 4. 6:37 5. A. 3:05 B. 4:40 6. 9:02
7. 11:50pm on Friday, 2nd October 1999 WK. Variable

28. 9 a. 11 b. 21 c. 25 d. 41 e. 21 f. 50 g. 203 WK. 12, 28, 4, 3

29. 1. 3000 2. 500 3. 4500 4. 0.75 5. 1.5 6. 30 7. 2.5 8. 0.5 9. 5 10. 160 11. 0.75 12. 1.9 13. (approx)200 - 500g
14. Variable 15. (approx) 10litres 16. 250ml (0.25l) 17. 36kg 18. 0.1m WK. 8000

30. 1. 1.4m or 140cm 2. a.36mm b.25mm 3. 1.1m 4. 269 5. 2.5kg 6. 200 7. 5 8. 6 9. 1.6m (160cm)
10. 2.75km(2 ³/₄ km) WK. 2.622km

31. 1. 15,16,17 2. 8 and 2 3. 24 4. All sides (and diagonals) add up to 15 5. 13 - 4 + 8 =17 6. 24 7. 13
8. 1,8 and 6 : 3,5 and 7 : 2,4 and 9 (There are others) WK. 150

32. 1. £10.95 2. 24 3. 21 4. 120 5. 372 6. 62 7. 3 8. 'The numbers are increasing by 5' etc WK. O(October),N,D.
The months!

33. 1. 2000,20000,200000 2. 500,50,5 3. 100 4. 100 5. £39 6. 100 7. 24 8. 1010g 9. 15 10. 1132km 11. 3,-1,-5,-9
12. 0.2, 2.2, 2.7, 7.2, 7.7 WK. ³/₄, 1³/₄

34. 1. Even 2. Odd 3. Even 4. Even 5. Odd 6. Odd 7. Odd 8. Even 9. ÷ (Divided) 10. – (Take away) 11. 155.5 12. 36
WK. £22.50

35. 1. 18 2. 14 cm 3. 8 cm 4. 12 cm WK.

36. 1. - 2. (Equilateral) Triangle 3. Hexagon 4. Octagon 5. (Isosceles) Triangle 6. Semi-circle 7. (Irregular) Hexagon 8. Heptagon 9. Tetrahedron (Triangular based pyramid) 10. a. Triangular prism b. Cuboid c. Cone d. Cylinder 11. 11
12. Cube WK. Triangular prism

37. 1. 2. 3. 1 (Vertical) 4. a. 1 b. 2 c. 0 d. 0 e. 2 f. 0 g. 5 h. 8 i. 1 j. 1 WK.

38. 1. (3,1) 2. A = (1,6) 3. B = (2,1) 4. C = (9,7) 5. (1,1),(2,2),(3,3),(4,4),(5,5),(6,6),(7,7) WK. SW (South-West)

39. 90 45 1. 4 2a. (approx) 45 b. (approx) 135 3. East 4a. 30 b. 60 c. 120 5. 30,45,60,180,360 6. 4, 3, 2, 1
7. WK. S

40. 1. 2. Thursday 3. Tuesday 4. 122 5. Rupinder,Sally,Tom,Meggie 6. Tom and Meggie 7.